This igloo book belongs to:

....

Contents

igloobooks

Published in 2016
by Igloo Books Ltd, Cottage Farm, Sywell, NN6 0BJ
www.igloobooks.com

Illustrated by Ruth Galloway
Written by Melanie Joyce

Designed by Justine Ablett
Edited by Jenny Cox

LEO002 0616
2 4 6 8 10 9 7 5 3 1
ISBN 978-1-78557-632-4

Printed and manufactured in China

5 Minute Tales
Dinosaur Stories

igloobooks

Time to Share

Once, there was a little dinosaur called Bonny
who had four best friends...

...Della...

...Donny...

... Spike...

... and Sid.

They had played together since they were baby dinosaurs
and their play days were great fun, until Bonny decided
that she didn't want to share.

"I want to wear the crown,"

said Bonny one day, when everyone was playing at Della's house.

She **snatched** the sparkly crown from Della and paraded around with it on her head.

"That's not very nice," said Spike, putting his arm round Della.

But Bonny didn't listen.

When everyone played pirates at Sid's house, Bonny insisted on being the captain and wouldn't share the special pirate clothes. She said the others could scrub the decks and walk the plank.

"I don't want to," said Sid, but Bonny wouldn't listen.

At the park, Bonny wouldn't wait her turn. She **squashed** onto the swing and **squished** onto the slide.

"I'm going first!" she cried, as she **whizzed** the roundabout round super-fast, then took up the whole of the sandpit.

Soon, it was time for a play day at Bonny's house. She got out her dressing-up box and her storybooks and her games.

"This is going to be fun,"

she said, as she waited for the doorbell to ring.

But the bell didn't ring.

Bonny waited and the clock **tick-ticked**, but still nobody came.
So Bonny went to see Mummy for a cuddle.

"It's because you won't share, Bonny," said Mummy.
"If you say sorry, that will put everything right."

So, Bonny phoned Della and
Donny and Spike and Sid.

"I'm Sorry.
Please come
and play,"

she said.

Everyone did come to play. They all had such fun with the dressing-up box and Bonny remembered to share all her toys.

"You can have the crown, Della,"

said Bonny.

"Thank you, Bonny,"

said Della, putting the sparkly crown on her head.

After that, Bonny and her friends **always** played nicely together. Bonny learned to share and sometimes, if she was very well behaved, she **even** got to be the queen!

11

Super Dino

"Help!" cried Dippy the Diplodocus, trying to climb out of the squelchy swamp. "I'm stuck!"

He **wriggled** and **jiggled**, but couldn't get out of the slime.

Suddenly, a red and blue blur streaked across the sky.

"It's Super Dino to the rescue!" shouted Dippy, waving madly at his hero.

Super Dino **swooped** down and plucked
the little dinosaur from the swamp,
splashing gloopy mud all over his cape.

"Thank you for saving me," said Dippy.
"You're welcome," replied Super Dino
and he shot off into the sky.

Terry the Pterodactyl was pecking juicy berries from the bush when his wings got caught in the **prickly** branches.

"Help me!"

shouted Terry,
struggling to get free.

ZOOM!

Super Dino **whizzed** to the rescue.

Spiky thorns **ripped** holes in Super Dino's cape, but he untangled the little Pterodactyl and **pulled** him free. Terry was so grateful he gave the superhero a hug, covering him in **sticky** berry juice.

"No problem,"

said Super Dino.

Then he took off into the clouds.

Next, Super Dino spotted Trixie the T-rex building a sandcastle on the beach. She didn't notice the tide coming in.

Suddenly, a **huge** wave **splashed** over her, leaving the little dino balancing on top of a rock.

"Help!"

she shrieked, as sandy water **swirled** around her feet.

With a **whoosh,** the superhero soared down and swept Trixie to safety.

Then he looked at his cape. It was covered in **slime**, **goo** and **sticky** sand. There was even a **big hole** in it.

"I can't be a superhero without a cape,"

said Super Dino, sadly. He took the cape off and dropped it to the ground.

As he **plodded** home, Super Dino heard someone calling from the top of a mountain.

"Help!
I can't get down,"

shouted Stevie
the Stegosaurus.

Super Dino **flew** to the mountain top and rescued Stevie, then he realised he wasn't wearing his cape. "Perhaps I don't need it after all," he thought.

"Hooray for Super Dino!"

cheered his friends, and they gave him a special present to say thank you for saving them. It was a new cape.

"I love it!"

cried Super Dino.

He knew he didn't need a cape to be a hero, but Super Dino was still happy to get such a **lovely** gift from his friends.

19

Bob and Barney

"I'm going next door to see Mrs Diplodocus," said Mum to Bob and Barney one day. "Aunt Betty is coming to visit later and I want this house to stay clean and tidy. No messing about, please."

"Alright!"

called Bob and Barney from the garden.

The brothers started **kicking** their football into a **muddy** puddle made by the leaky hose.

"Bet I can kick it further than you,"

said Bob.

"Bet you can't,"

replied Barney, as Bob booted the ball.

ThWACK!

It shot over Barney's head and **flew** towards the house.

The back door **swung** open and the ball **bounced** inside.

"Bet I can get to it faster than you,"

said Bob.

"Bet you can't,"

replied Barney.

The two of them **stomped** towards the back door
and tried to **squash** through it at the same time.

Bob wriggled free and **stomped** to get the ball.
"Tackle!" cried Barney, as he **slid** across
the floor. He grabbed Bob by the feet.

"I'm stronger
than you!"

he shouted.

"No you aren't,"

said Bob.

He **thrashed** his
legs and **kicked**
the ball up onto
the bookcase.

"Bet I can jump higher than you," said Bob.

"Bet you can't," said Barney.

The two of them **bounced** up and down until the floor **shook**, the furniture **shook** and the pictures **fell** off the walls.

Ding, dong!
The doorbell rang.
Aunt Betty was early.
"Come in," said Bob
and Barney, sheepishly.

When Aunt Betty saw the state
of the house, she gasped.
"We better get this cleaned
up before your mother comes
home," she said. "You two
have got to work together or
you'll be in **big** trouble."

25

So, Bob got the bucket and Barney got the mop.
"You wash and I'll dry," said Bob.
Soon, the muddy bounce marks
and footprints were cleaned up.

Bob vacuumed and Barney tidied up.
Pictures were hung on the walls and
furniture turned the right way up.

Together, Bob and Barney got the ball down from the bookcase. "Well done," said Aunt Betty. "You've finished just in time." Mum came into the room and smiled. "How did you two keep the house so tidy?" she asked.

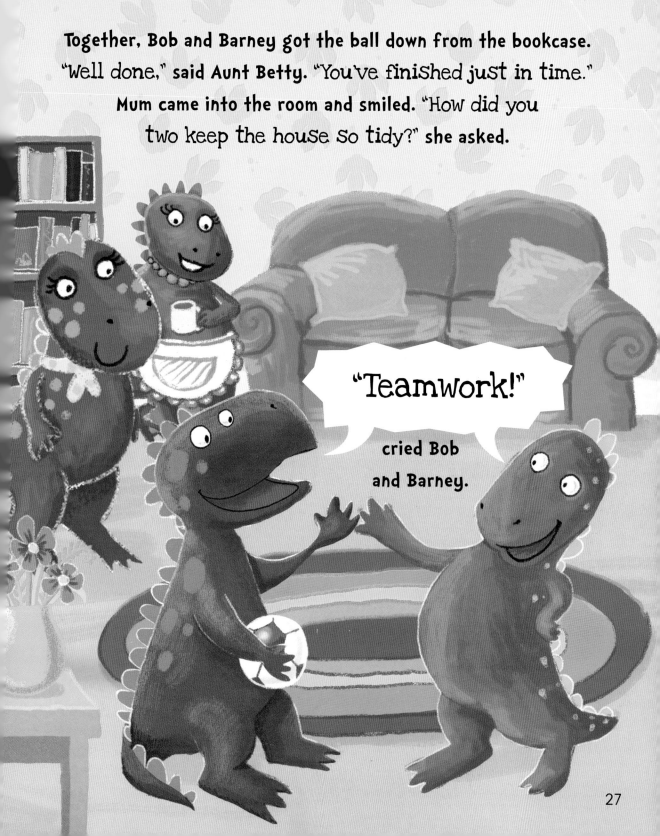

"Teamwork!"

cried Bob and Barney.

"I've lost another tooth! Look, I got a gold coin!"

cried Tommy the Pterodactyl one day.

He flew around **excitedly**, showing the coin to all of his friends.

Everyone **cheered** and smiled, except Tyrone the Tyrannosaurus. He kept his mouth firmly **shut**.

Tyrone was embarrassed because he hadn't lost any baby teeth yet.
He wanted a gap like Tommy and his other friends, Steggie and Pete.
Their big teeth were coming through already.

"It's not fair,"

grumbled Tyrone, as his
friends gathered round.

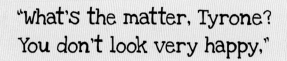

"What's the matter, Tyrone?
You don't look very happy,"

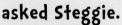

asked Steggie.

"This is the matter,"

replied Tyrone.

He opened his mouth to reveal two rows of tiny teeth.

"It's not your fault
you've still got your
baby teeth,"

said Steggie,
trying not to giggle.

Tyrone wasn't happy at all.

"I'll show them," he thought.

He **stomped** off back home to figure out what to do.

No one took him seriously with tiny teeth. Why couldn't **just one** fall out? If only he could speed things up a little.

31

Mum said that Tyrone's teeth would probably start to fall out when he was **crunching** something.

"That's it!"

cried Tyrone.

He **gnawed** on nuts...

... and **chewed** on branches...

... but nothing did any good.

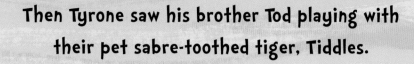
Then Tyrone saw his brother Tod playing with their pet sabre-toothed tiger, Tiddles.

"Even Tiddles has got bigger teeth than me. It's not fair,"

thought Tyrone.

So he got the **biggest** boulder he could find, and he was just about to take a **big bite** of it when...

"Oh no you don't," **said Dad.** "You can't force your teeth to fall out, Tyrone. They will come out when they are ready to. You just need to be patient. I promise you that your grown-up teeth will be worth waiting for."

After that, Dad watched Tyrone so closely, he stopped **waggling** his tooth altogether.

Then, one day Tyrone was eating a nice crunchy apple and guess what?

His tooth fell out!

Then another...

...and another.

Soon, all of Tyrone's baby teeth had gone. And that wasn't all.

Not only did Tyrone have a pile of gold coins, before long
he had a brand-new set of pearly white teeth. They were so
impressive, his friends nicknamed him **Gnashers**.
No one dared laugh at Tyrone now and he **loved** it.

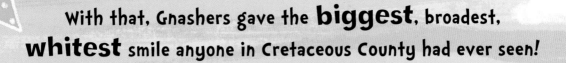

With that, Gnashers gave the **biggest**, broadest, **whitest** smile anyone in Cretaceous County had ever seen!

"Thanks, Mum and Dad. You were right, my teeth were definitely worth waiting for."

said Tyrone.

Dino and Caveboy

ROAR! went Derek the dinosaur excitedly one morning.

"Can we go to Prehistoric Park? Pleeease?"

he asked.

"Yes, but stay close," replied Dad. "The **big** volcano is near there and it's dangerous. There are cavemen, too. They are unfriendly and **don't** like dinosaurs."

"Yes, but don't wander off," replied Dad. The **big** volcano might erupt, or you might meet a dinosaur. They're grumpy and **don't** like cavemen."

At the park, Derek and Clod went on lots of rides.

Afterwards, Derek asked Dad for a swamp burger.
"Alright," said Dad. "Wait here, and don't go near the volcano."

Derek waited, but Dad had to queue
for ages to get a swamp burger.

Meanwhile, not far away...

Clod climbed off the ghost train.

"Can I have a swamp cone, please?" he asked.

"Alright," said Dad. "Wait here, and keep away from the volcano."

"Okay,"

said Clod, **thumping** his club on the ground.

41

Derek got tired too, and also wandered off.
The volcano **rumbled** and the ground

shook.

Clod **ran** and Derek **ran**, too.

Clod **scrambled** up a tree and Derek **jumped** into a hole, except it wasn't a hole. It was a swamp! The volcano spat sparks. It was about to blow and Derek was stuck.

"Please help me. Get my dad! He's like me, but bigger,"

cried Derek.

"Okay!"

said Clod, as he ran off.

Meanwhile, the two dads were searching for their sons, when...

"Dinosaur!"

"Caveman!"

"Help!"

cried Clod.

In the swamp, Derek was disappearing into the **gloopy slime.**

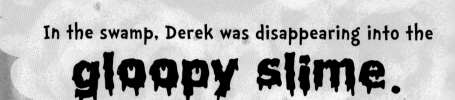

"We've got to work together,"

said Clod's dad.

So, everyone **pulled** and **shoved**...

... and **shoved** and **pulled.**

At last, Derek **flopped** out of the swamp, just as there was the most almighty **BLAST!**

Derek and his dad were **very** grateful to Clod and his dad.
They agreed that it was silly for dinosaurs and cavemen to
dislike each other when they could actually be friends.

So after that, Clod and Derek
played together every day.

Their dads became **friends** too, and before long cavemen
and dinosaurs were having prehistoric **parties** together.

At last, everyone was **happy** in the land of the dinosaurs.

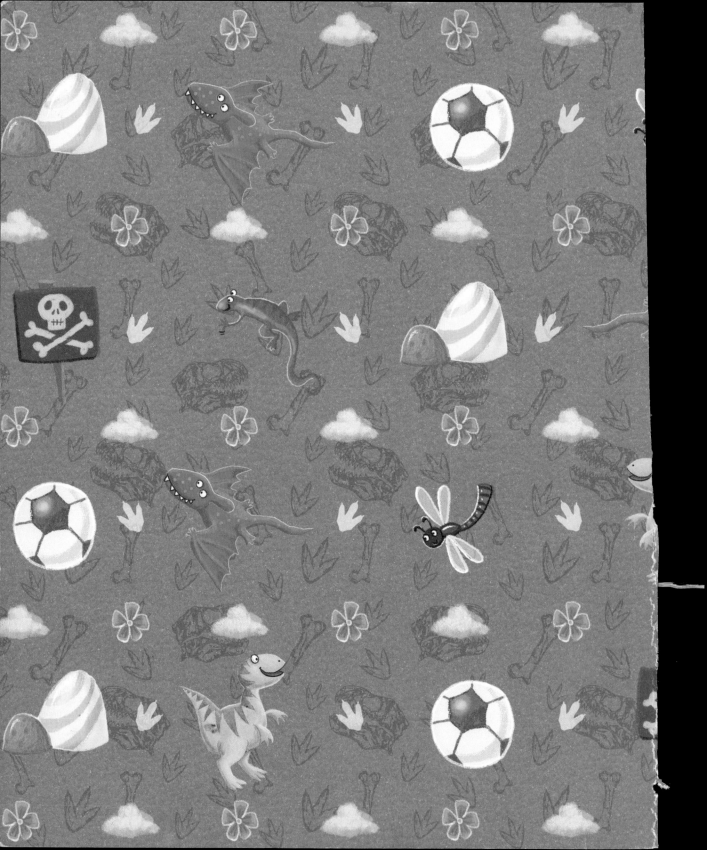